To:

K

From:

First published in paperback in Great Britain by HarperCollins Children's Books in 2009

1 3 5 7 9 10 8 6 4 2

ISBN-13: 978-0-00-730755-5

HarperCollins Children's Books is a division of HarperCollins Publishers Ltd.

Illustrations copyright © HarperCollins Publishers Ltd 2009

Visit our website at: www.harpercollins.co.uk

Printed and bound in China

FIVE LITTLE
PUMPKINS

Illustrated by Ben Mantle

HarperCollins *Children's Books*

Five little pumpkins
sitting on a gate.

Pumpkin
Patch

The second one said,
"There are witches in the air!"

The third one said,

"Good folk, beware!"

The fourth one said,
"We'll run...

...and run!"

The fifth one said,
"Let's have some fun!"

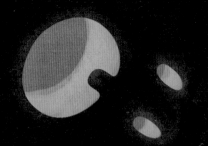

...and OUT

went the light...

...and the
five little pumpkins
rolled...

...out of sight!